SNAIL'S SILLY ADVENTURES

SNAIL'S SILLY ADVENTURES

Previously published as two separate books, titled *Snail Has Lunch* and *Snail Finds a Home*

by MARY PETERSON

ALADDIN

NEW YORK   LONDON   TORONTO   SYDNEY   NEW DELHI

ALADDIN

An imprint of Simon & Schuster Children's Publishing Division
1230 Avenue of the Americas, New York, New York 10020
This Aladdin edition October 2020
Copyright © 2016, 2020 by Mary Peterson
All rights reserved, including the right of reproduction in whole or in part in any form.
ALADDIN and related logo are registered trademarks of Simon & Schuster, Inc.
For information about special discounts for bulk purchases, please contact
Simon & Schuster Special Sales at 1-866-506-1949 or business@simonandschuster.com.
The Simon & Schuster Speakers Bureau can bring authors to your live event. For more information
or to book an event contact the Simon & Schuster Speakers Bureau at 1-866-248-3049
or visit our website at www.simonspeakers.com.
Designed by Karina Granda and Tiara Iandiorio
The illustrations for this book were rendered digitally.
The text of this book was set in Archer Book.
Manufactured in China 0920 SCP
2 4 6 8 10 9 7 5 3 1
Library of Congress Control Number 2019948054
ISBN 978-1-5344-6345-5 (hc)
ISBN 978-1-5344-6344-8 (pbk)
ISBN 978-1-5344-7562-5 (eBook)
This book was previously published as two separate books,
titled *Snail Has Lunch* and *Snail Finds a Home*.
ISBN 978-1-5344-9480-0 (Literati proprietary edition)

For my adventuresome girls, J and P

CHAPTER 1

Snail lived in a bucket.

He loved his old rusty bucket.

WARM IN
WINTER

COOL IN
SUMMER

DRY WHEN
IT RAINS

AND CHOCK-FULL OF
BROWN GRASS AND DIRT

He was so comfy he had no reason
to leave his bucket.

Ever.

Mmmm.
Bland.

Nearly every afternoon, Snail's friend Ladybug would come by. Sometimes she would tell him stories about her friends . . .

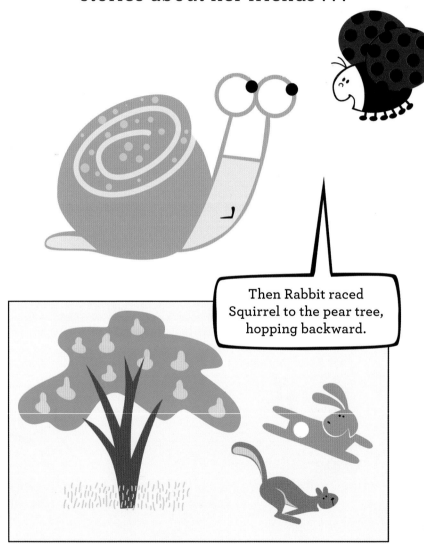

Then Rabbit raced Squirrel to the pear tree, hopping backward.

or stories about the newest
tasty treat in the garden. . . .

Every visit, Ladybug would try to convince Snail to leave his bucket.

Would you like to come in and have some brown grass and dirt with me?

IN? Brown grass and dirt?

Snail, the sun is shining!

The pea pods are crunchy!

The birds are chirping!

The strawberries are super-sweet!

13

THINKING.

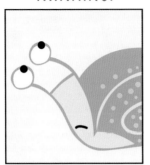

PONDERING.

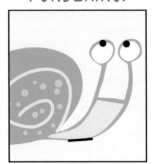

CONSIDERING.

RUMINATING.

Ladybug was disappointed
and went on her way.

15

Snail would soon find out.

CHAPTER 2

Snail had no idea what had happened.

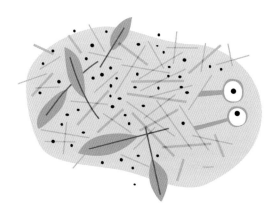

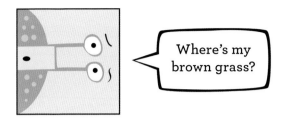

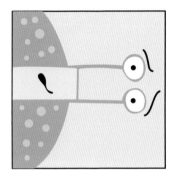

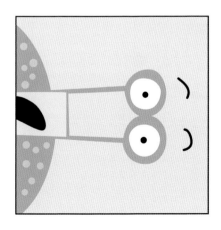

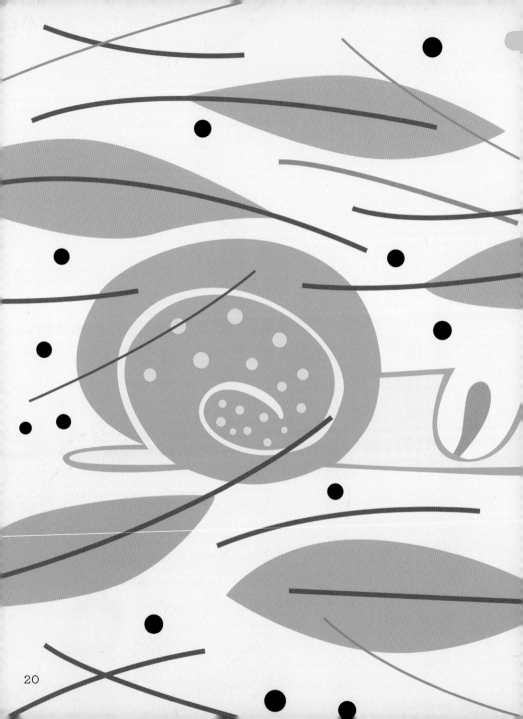

Just then a shadow passed over Snail's face.

He shut his eyes tight, hoping it would disappear.

Relax, Snail! It's just me.

Snail opened his eyes and saw his best friend.

But Snail wouldn't budge. There was only one place he wanted to go: **HOME!**

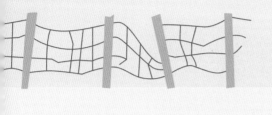

Snail was scared.
But he was also hungry.

Wait
for me!

Slowly but not so surely,
he followed Ladybug from . . .

some
flowerpots . . .

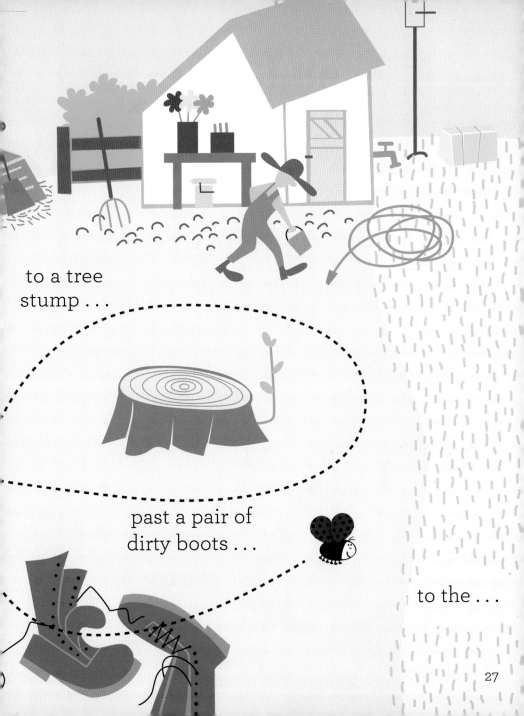

to a tree
stump...

past a pair of
dirty boots...

to the...

27

CHAPTER 3

Garden!

Snail couldn't believe his eyes.
Everything was so colorful.

But the rhubarb was . . .

At that moment a bunch of little red
something-or-others caught Snail's eye.

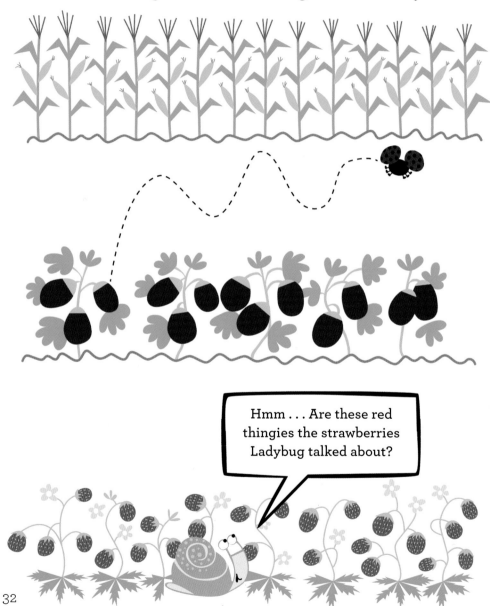

Hmm . . . Are these red
thingies the strawberries
Ladybug talked about?

Since this was Snail's first time in the garden, he didn't know Ladybug was only one row over.

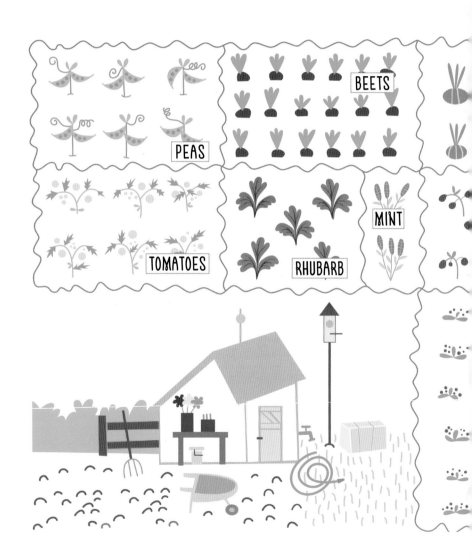

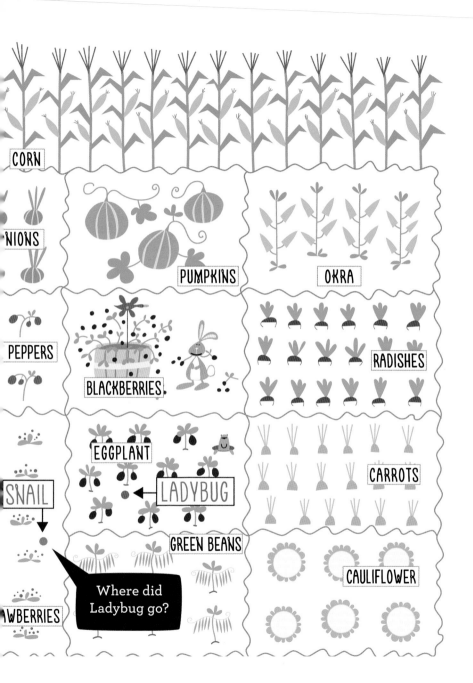

CORN

NIONS

PUMPKINS

OKRA

PEPPERS

BLACKBERRIES

RADISHES

EGGPLANT

SNAIL

LADYBUG

CARROTS

GREEN BEANS

Where did Ladybug go?

WBERRIES

CAULIFLOWER

Snail looked under the green beans,

inside the cauliflower,

and around the carrots.

Will I ever see Ladybug again?

And then he looked up right into . . .

CHAPTER 4

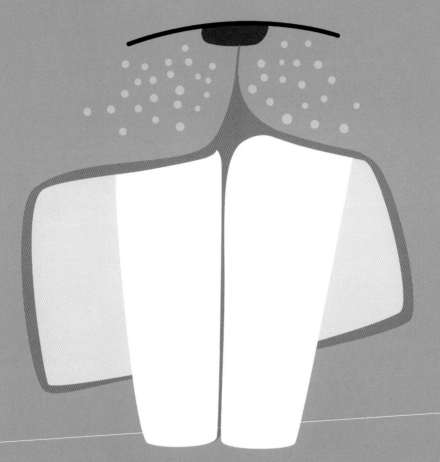

Two big teeth.

For the second time that day,
Snail closed his eyes.

39

Snail couldn't believe how Gopher stuffed his cheeks.

When Gopher was finally finished, Snail asked . . .

Snail looked past Gopher and saw another furry creature. This one was bigger and had long ears.

What a ridiculous question. There must be fifteen buckets in this garden.

BIG ROUND ORANGE BUCKET

SMALL RED BUCKET WITH A HOLE

STORAGE BUCKET WITH A SNAP LID

USED PAINT BUCKET

WOODEN WATER BUCKET

OLD RUSTY BUCKET

Snail's eyes got wide.

Did you say "old rusty bucket"?

Rabbit took a bite from a blackberry.

Snail was about to cry.

46

It's just past the pumpkins. I'll take you there after this last bite.

Snail grinned from eyeball to eyeball.

Soon he would be home. And he hoped Ladybug would be there waiting for him.

CHAPTER 5

When Rabbit finished his blackberries,
he quickly led the way. Snail moved as fast
as he could, but he was a snail, after all.

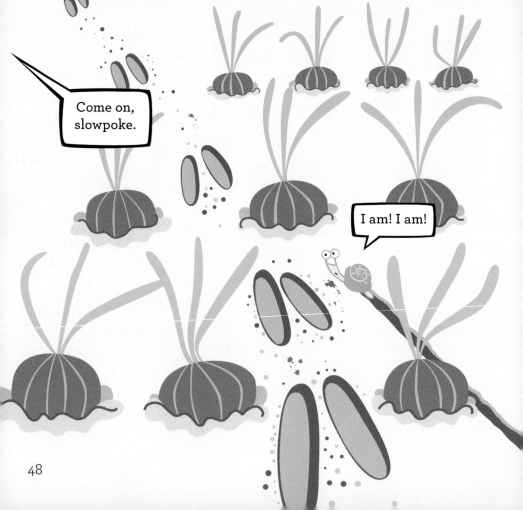

Right past the onions, another pretty little red strawberry appeared in front of him.

Now, if Snail had ever left his cozy little bucket, he would have known that was not a sweet and delicious strawberry.

What he was about to eat . . .

was a pretty little RED HOT PEPPER.

53

Be careful with the pretty little peppers. They may be cute, but they are spicy!

Snail was not happy.

55

Ladybug was shocked.

57

Maybe Ladybug had a point. Snail looked dreamily toward the strawberry patch and couldn't believe his eyes.

Ladybug, LOOK! There's my bucket!

Snail and Ladybug climb on Rabbit's back . . .

and in one,

two,

three hops,

they were at the bucket.

Snail was confused.
The bucket was old and
rusty, but it was filled wit

STRAWBERRIES!

Wait a minute.
Whose bucket is this?

It's yours, silly.

Oh, Snail!

CHAPTER 6

Now, as much as Snail loved
his old rusty bucket...

he loved strawberries even more.
Day after day, he ate strawberries
for all his meals.

BREAKFAST

LUNCH

SUPPER

AND DESSERT

69

Every day, Snail's best friend,
Ladybug, came to visit. And every day,
she would ask the same question.

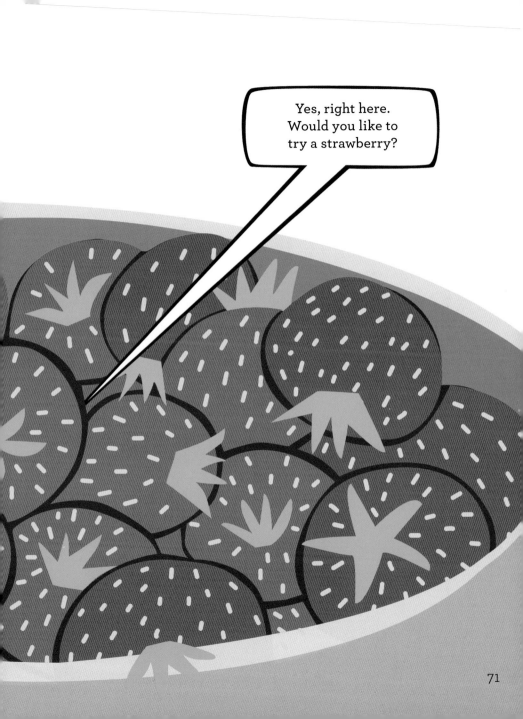

Ladybug was always trying to convince
Snail that he couldn't live in a rusty
bucket eating strawberries forever.

I found some cute homes
for you near my house.
How about we
check them out?

Why?
I have everything
I love right here.

Sweet red strawberries
in an old rusty bucket.

Ladybug left disappointed.
But she was not a quitter.
Tomorrow she would try again.

73

The next day, as usual, Ladybug was back. And she couldn't believe her eyes. Snail had eaten so many sweet **RED** strawberries, he had turned **GREEN**.

My tummy hurts.

Before Snail could answer . . .

he threw up.

77

CHAPTER 7

Early the next morning, Ladybug met Snail with a long list of places to visit.

Snail followed Ladybug to the top of a fence post.
In the distance, he spied an apple orchard.

While Ladybug checked her list, Snail
slimed down the fence post and . . .

wandered in the direction
of the apple orchard.

BIRDBATH

ROCK

HONEYSUCKLE

TRASH
CAN

GOPHER
HOLE

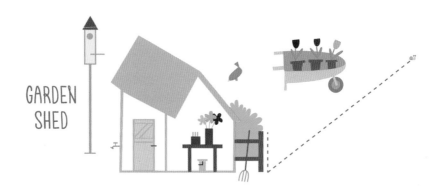

GARDEN
SHED

APPLE ORCHARD

BEEHIVE

CHICKEN COOP

DOGHOUSE

AMBROSIA

Now, if Snail had ever seen a chicken or a chicken coop, he would have known this was excellent advice. But he hadn't, so he didn't.

CHAPTER 8

Ladybug led Snail to her
favorite honeysuckle bush.

Just then, Snail and Ladybug
heard a familiar voice.

Good morning, friends.
May I suggest something
a bit more sheltered?

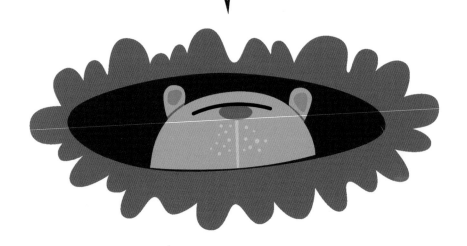

91

Ladybug continued to show Snail
the different spots on her list.
Snail continued to find problems with each one.

93

95

While Ladybug, Gopher, and Rabbit looked for Ladybug's lost list, pretty red thingies once again caught Snail's eye.

Forgetting Ladybug's warning, Snail wandered off in the direction of the apple orchard.

CHAPTER 9

Suddenly, a fellow stepped onto the path.
His bright red hat made Snail smile.

Hello, Snail.

Hello.
Who are you?

Ladybug and I are dear friends.
She asked me to show you some
other special homes, including
the apple orchard.

Apple?
What's an
apple?

Snail was happy to follow
Ladybug's helpful friend with
the beautiful red hat. They headed
around the back of a little shed.

But when they got to the back of the shed, the fellow in the red hat stopped, causing Snail to run SMACK into his leg.

Snail couldn't help but take a close-up look.

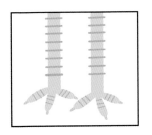

YELLOW LEGS

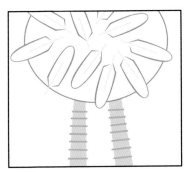

WHITE FEATHERS

POINTY BEAK

CHICKEN!!!

GULP!

Chicken grinned at Snail.

Well, it was nice meeting you, Mr. . . . um . . . I must be going.

Maybe we can hang out sometime. Later. Hard to say when. I'm in between homes.

Chicken licked his beak.

You're hungry! Me too!

I saw a nice patch of corn just back there. Corn is tasty, unlike snails. **Snails are gross.**

YUCK!

Chicken leaned in close.

Thank you for coming for lunch, Snail!

Meanwhile, back at Ambrosia Acres . . .

115

CHAPTER 10

Chicken snatched Snail into his beak.

120

Snail couldn't stay
angry for long, because
lying next to him was
a bright red apple
on a pile of brown
grass and dirt.

Snail couldn't
help himself.

He took a bite.

123

Mary Peterson is an illustrator of many books for young readers, including *Dig In!*, *Piggies in the Pumpkin Patch*, *Wiggle and Waggle*, *Wooby & Peep*, *Snail Has Lunch,* and *Snail Finds a Home*. She lives in Los Angeles, California.

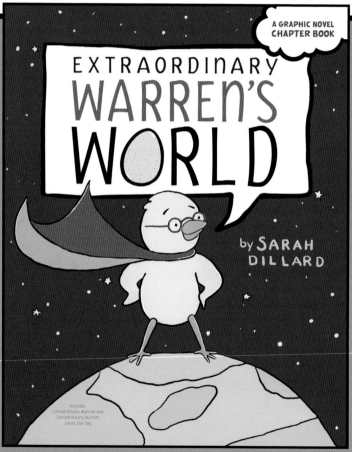